ROD SERLING's THE TWILIGHT ZONE

THE AFTER HOURS

Adaptation from Rod Serling's original script by

MARK KNEECE

Illustrated by

REBEKAH ISAACS

BLOOMSBURY

LONDON BERLIN NEW YORK

INTRODUCTION

There is a fifth dimension beyond that which is known to man. It is a dimension as vast as space and timeless as infinity. It is the middle ground between light and shadow, between science and superstition, and it lies between the pit of man's fears and the summit of his knowledge. This is the dimension of imagination. It is an area which we call the Twilight Zone.

America, between the 1950s and early 1960s, was itself in a sort of "twilight zone." Following the victories of World War II and the attending economic boom—but before the Civil Rights marches; the assassinations of John F. Kennedy, Martin Luther King, Jr., and Robert F. Kennedy; and the Vietnam War—we were wrapped in a gleaming package of shining chrome, white picket fences, and Hollywood glamour. But beneath this shimmering facade lay a turbulent core of racial inequality, sexual inequality, and the Cold War threat of nuclear attacks from the Soviet Union. We'd never been more affluent—or more frightened.

Enter Rodman Edward Serling of Binghamton, New York. Serling began writing in his teens for his high school newspaper; as a student at Antioch College, he was already selling scripts to radio programs. While serving as a paratrooper in the U.S. Army Eleventh Airborne (for which he earned a Purple Heart), he wrote for the Armed Services Radio. He went on to write for film and television, first in feature presentations for *Hallmark Hall of Fame* and *Playhouse 90*, including the lauded "Requiem for a Heavyweight," perhaps drawing inspiration from his own experiences as a Golden Gloves boxer. More than two hundred of his teleplays were produced. In all, his work would win not only the adoration of listeners and viewers but a host of prestigious awards, including a record-breaking six Emmy awards—two of them for his greatest achievement, *The Twilight Zone*.

The worlds and characters presented over the course of five seasons, beginning in October 1959, were like nothing audiences had seen before. Television, the new "must have" appliance for America's increasingly prosperous households, offered comedies such as *I Love Lucy* and *The Honeymooners*, news programs including Edward R. Murrow's *See It Now*, as well as Westerns, game shows, and soap operas. With a typewriter as his spade, Serling dug beneath the surface of the expected and planted the seeds of a more imaginative and thoughtful genre, writing more than half of the show's 156 episodes while producing and hosting all of them. He bravely took on themes of oppression, prejudice, and paranoia, all the while giving people what they needed at the end of the day: entertainment.

While he had his run-ins with censorship, Serling's clever use of other worlds and veiled scenarios generally protected him. As he explained, what he couldn't have a Republican or a Democrat espouse on the show, he could have an alien profess without offending the sponsors. This approach also allowed viewers to take away whatever message best suited them; the more reflective could consider the psychological and political implications, while others might be satisfied with simply enjoying the thrill of the surface story. So much more than mere science fiction or fantasy, Serling's scripts are parables that explore the multifaceted natures of hope, fear, humanity, loneliness, and self-delusion.

Half a century later, *The Twilight Zone* remains a part of our culture, routinely referenced in print and on television, having become a shorthand expression that succinctly describes the bizarre and unexpected. The original episodes are still aired on the SciFi Channel, both in late-night slots and as day-long marathons. The show was literally a Who's Who of Hollywood, helping to foster the careers of fledgling actors including Robert Redford, Ron Howard, Dennis Hopper, Charles Bronson, and William Shatner. It has also inspired countless authors and filmmakers, who have gone on to break through boundaries of their own.

In the fifty years since *The Twilight Zone* first aired, we've faced new enemies and have altered our definitions of happiness, but our core hopes and fears remain the same, as does our desire to be entertained. The stories are as compelling, and as telling, as ever. And now, in their newest incarnation, Serling's scripts serve as the basis for this graphic novel series, which honors the original text and even echoes the storyboarding of television, but offers a fresh interpretation, as seen through the eyes of a new generation of artists.

—Anna Marlis Burgard
Director of Industry Partnerships, Savannah College of Art and Design

You're traveling through
another dimension,
a dimension not only of sight and sound
but of mind;
a journey into a wondrous land
whose boundaries
are that of imagination.
That's the signpost up ahead—
your next stop,
the Twilight Zone!

...THE TWILIGHT ZONE!

SCRUFF
SCRUFF
SCRUFF

MAY I HELP YOU?

?!?

OVER HERE.

I'M SORRY. YOU LOOKED AS IF YOU MIGHT NEED SOME HELP.

CAN I HELP YOU?

NO, THANK YOU.

BUT...

THAT'S NOT WHAT I WAS LOOKING FOR.

...IN LADIES' WEAR PLEASE.

BING

OH, I'M SOR...

...RY.

BUMP!

GOING UP, MA'AM?

GOING UP, MA'AM?

?

THIS ISN'T WHERE I'M SUPPOSED TO BE...

WAS SOMEONE HELPING YOU?

CAN I SHOW YOU SOMETHING?

I...I WAS LOOKING...

I WAS LOOKING FOR A GOLD THIMBLE.

A GIFT...

...FOR MY MOTHER

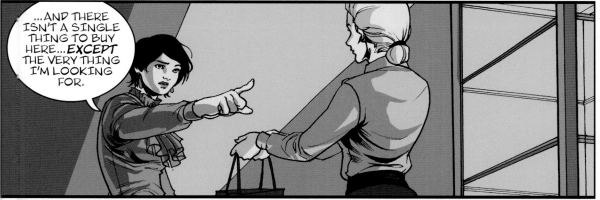

I BEG YOUR PARDON?

RRRR...

AM I WHAT?

AM I HAPPY??

RRRR...

RRRR...

YOU'LL FORGIVE ME, BUT...IT'S REALLY NONE OF **YOUR** BUSINESS.

RRRR...

RRRR...

REALLY? IT'S NONE OF MY BUSINESS?

ALL RIGHT, MISS WHITE. SUIT YOURSELF.

RRRR...

YOU CAN'T KNOW ANYTHING ABOUT ME.

RRRR...

BANG

RIGHT. IT'S **NONE** OF MY BUSINESS.

GOING DOWN.

...I DISTINCTLY TOLD HER THAT IF THE ITEM WERE DAMAGED, WE WOULD MAKE IT GOOD—EITHER BY REPLACEMENT OR REFUND. I DISTINCTLY TOLD HER THAT, MR. SLOAN.

THEN WHAT'S THE PROBLEM, MR. ARMBRUSTER?

SHE HAS SOME IDIOTIC STORY ABOUT HAVING PURCHASED THE THIMBLE IN QUESTION ON THE *EIGHTEENTH FLOOR.*

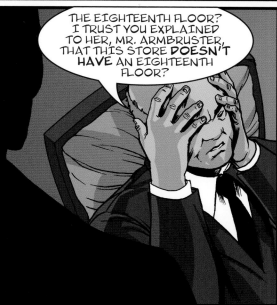

THE EIGHTEENTH FLOOR? I TRUST YOU EXPLAINED TO HER, MR. ARMBRUSTER, THAT THIS STORE **DOESN'T HAVE** AN EIGHTEENTH FLOOR?

MR. SLOAN, BELIEVE ME, SIR, I HAVE TRIED DESPERATELY— I REALLY MEAN DESPERATELY— TO ACQUAINT HER WITH THIS FACT...

AND...?

SIGH

SHE INSISTS SHE WAS TAKEN UP TO THE EIGHTEENTH FLOOR, WAITED ON BY A RATHER ODD WOMAN—AND FURTHERMORE THAT SHE WAS TAKEN THERE IN AN ELEVATOR WITH A STRANGE OPERATOR...

OPERATOR? FOR THE ELEVATOR? WE HAVEN'T HAD ONE OF THOSE SINCE 1957...

IT'S BEEN ALMOST THIRTY MINUTES. ARE YOU SURE SHE DOESN'T NEED AN AMBULANCE?

WE CAN'T JUST LEAVE HER IN THE ALTERATIONS ROOM ALL NIGHT.

I'M SURE SHE JUST NEEDS TO REST A BIT. SHE SEEMED MORE DISTURBED ABOUT SOMETHING THAN INJURED.

I COULDN'T AGREE MORE. THAT WOMAN IS CERTAINLY DISTURBED.

WE SHOULD EJECT HER FROM THE STORE IMMEDIATELY. SHE CLAIMED TO HAVE SEEN AN AD FOR GOLD THIMBLES. RIDICULOUS!

YES, I DON'T RECOLLECT US RUNNING SUCH AN AD.

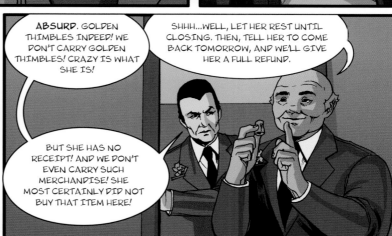

ABSURD. GOLDEN THIMBLES INDEED! WE DON'T CARRY GOLDEN THIMBLES! CRAZY IS WHAT SHE IS!

BUT SHE HAS NO RECEIPT! AND WE DON'T EVEN CARRY SUCH MERCHANDISE! SHE MOST CERTAINLY DID NOT BUY THAT ITEM HERE!

SHHH...WELL, LET HER REST UNTIL CLOSING. THEN, TELL HER TO COME BACK TOMORROW, AND WE'LL GIVE HER A FULL REFUND.

WE DON'T NEED BAD PUBLICITY, MR. ARMBRUSTER.

AND...WE DON'T WANT HER GETTING ANY IDEAS ABOUT LAWSUITS WITH REGARD TO THE INCIDENT.

THE INCIDENT! BUT...

OF COURSE, MR. SLOAN.

MISS MAI! I WANT YOU TO SEE TO IT THAT THE YOUNG WOMAN IS COMFORTABLE. UNDERSTOOD?

SURE. SHE'LL BE ALL RIGHT, MR. ARMBRUSTER.

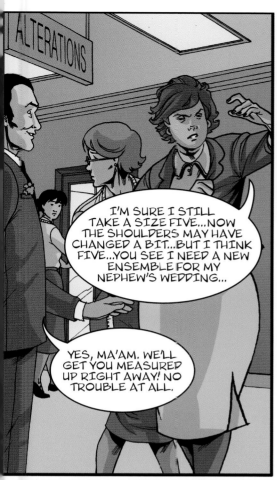

HELLO?

PLEASE... SOMEONE?

MR. SLOAN?

I'M LOCKED IN HERE.

IF ANYONE'S
OUT THERE...

...COULD
YOU PLEASE
HELP ME!

clicka click!

I MUST GET OUT.

MARSHA...

MARSHA...

WHO SAID THAT? WHO'S THERE?

Brinnng Brinnng!

A PHONE.

Brinnng Brinnng!

NNNT...

COME ON, DEAR...CLIMB OFF IT.

YOU REMEMBER, MARSHA?

YOU KNOW WHO YOU ARE.

STOP IT.

RATTLE
RATTLE
RATTLE...

Bing!

MARSHA!

MARSHA!

MARSHA!

MARSHA!

clack

NRRRrrr...

NO...

rrrrr...

OH NO. NO NO! DOWN! NOT UP! DOWN!

clck clck clikity clck

rrrrr...1

SOB NO! *SOB* I DON'T WANT TO *SOB* GO THERE! *SOB*...

IT'S IN BITS AND PIECES, LIKE A DREAM.

LET ME SEE...

THERE WERE PEOPLE...LOTS AND LOTS OF PEOPLE...

THEIR MOVEMENTS, SO QUICK AND PURPOSEFUL...

...THE WAY SHOPPERS GET AT CLOSING TIME ON HOLIDAYS.

...AND I WANTED TO SHOP, TOO...

...AND I REMEMBER... WHAT IT FEELS LIKE TO NOT BE ONE OF THEM...NOT TO HAVE ANYTHING...THAT WE DON'T TAKE ANYTHING WITH US OUT THERE...

NOT EVERYBODY TALKS LIKE MR. SLOAN.

BUT SOME PEOPLE ARE KIND.

KINDER EVEN THAN MR. SLOAN.

SUDDENLY YOU DO FEEL IT... YOU FEEL LIKE YOU BELONG... LIKE YOU REALLY WERE ONE OF THEM.

TO FEEL LIKE THAT... LIKE ONE OF THE OUTSIDERS...

...WHEN IT'S SO NICE... ONE FORGETS EVERYTHING WHEN THAT HAPPENS.

I FORGOT WHO I WAS...

...IT'S HARD TO EXPLAIN... BUT IT WAS PLEASANT...

IN THE STORE IT'S ALWAYS THE SAME... OPENING, CLOSING, STAYING PUT...

...ONLY... IT'S NOT SAFE TO FORGET.

JED JO AUTO SA

"our loss is your 9 765-2340

BRIMBLE
Great Gift!
Gold Thimble
Only $22.80

Select Sewing Notions

50-60 Off!

SPEEDEE MAID SERVICE

OUT THERE...

...THINGS ALWAYS CHANGE...

...SOMETHING HAPPENS...

...YOU DON'T KNOW **HOW** IT HAPPENS...

...AND IT DOESN'T MAKE SENSE...

...YOU JUST WATCH...

...AS EVERYTHING TURNS INTO SOMETHING ELSE...

...AND THEN IT JUST ALL ENDS.

SOMEONE IS A FRIEND...

...THEN THEY STOP AND THEY'RE STILL...

...AND YOU WONDER IF YOU'RE SUPPOSED TO DO SOMETHING.

AND YOU THINK ABOUT IT A LITTLE...

...YOU WAIT TO SEE WHAT HAPPENS...

...YOU WAIT...

...BUT THEN YOU START TO FORGET THEY WERE FRIENDLY ONCE...

Call Your Mother She Worries

MEOW?

...AND YOU TRY TO REMEMBER WHAT YOU WERE WAITING ON.

I WAS SUPPOSED TO DO SOMETHING...

...BUT I COULDN'T THINK WHAT.

THEN I SAW THE AD...

...AND I CAME IN...TO GET SOMETHING FOR...MY...MY MOTHER.

I REMEMBERED THAT I'D HAVE TO PAY FOR IT...

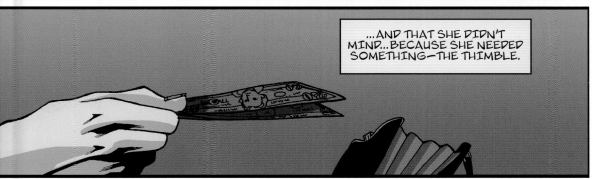

...AND THAT SHE DIDN'T MIND...BECAUSE SHE NEEDED SOMETHING—THE THIMBLE.

BUT I HAD COMPLETELY FORGOTTEN...

...WHO I REALLY AM...

CHK

...FOR A MOMENT.

MEOW?

AND WHEN I CAME IN THERE WAS SOMETHING ON MY DRESS... AND I TRIED TO REMEMBER AGAIN.

BUT NOW I KNOW... I'M A MANNEQUIN.

I'M A MANNEQUIN. AND IT WAS MY TURN TO...

YOUR TURN TO LEAVE US FOR A MONTH. SEE, MARSHA.

YOU JUST NEEDED TO RETRACE YOUR STEPS. BECOMING MUCH CLEARER NOW, ISN'T IT?

IT'S ALL THE MOVING AROUND... AND OUTSIDERS DO STRANGE THINGS...

...IT'S EASY TO FORGET EVERYTHING...

...TO THINK YOU'RE ONE OF THEM.

YOU WERE DUE BACK TWO WEEKS AGO, AND YOU DIDN'T SHOW UP.

AND YOU KNOW, MARSHA, THAT'S SELFISH, MY DEAR.

YES. OF COURSE.

ALL OF US WAIT OUR TURN.

WE SIMPLY DO NOT OVERSTAY IT.

I'M SORRY. I WON'T FORGET AGAIN.

IT WAS MY TURN STARTING TWO WEEKS AGO. I'M DELAYED ALREADY.

I'M SORRY.

OH, MR. ARMBRUSTER! WAS THAT YOUNG WOMAN FROM LAST NIGHT—THE ONE WITH THE THIMBLE—TAKEN CARE OF?

WHY YES, MR. SLOAN. I BELIEVE SHE WAS!

GOOD. WE PRIDE OURSELVES ON HAPPY CUSTOMERS, MR. ARMBRUSTER!

OF COURSE, MR. SLOAN. THANK YOU, SIR.

MISS MAI?

YES, SIR?

THAT YOUNG WOMAN WHO WAS LYING DOWN LAST NIGHT. DID SHE RETURN TO THE WORLD FROM WHENCE SHE CAME?

ER...YES, MR. ARMBRUSTER... THAT IS, SHE, SHE'S GONE.

GOOD! THEN I HOPE SHE HAS GONE VERY FAR AWAY!

LADIES! LADIES! THERE ISN'T TIME! TAKE YOUR PLACES AT ONCE!

I'M EXPECTING HUNDREDS OF DOLLARS IN SALES FROM EACH OF YOU BEFORE LUNCHTIME, UNDERSTAND?

YES, SIR.

?

!?!

The After Hours

Season One, Episode #34

Original Air Date: June 10, 1960

Written by Rod Serling

Cast

Narrator: Rod Serling

Marsha White: Anne Francis *
*Also appeared in *Jess-Belle* as the title character

Saleswoman: Elizabeth Allen

Mr. Armbruster: James Millhollin*
*Also appeared in *I Dream of Genie* as Masters
and *Mr. Dingle, the Strong* as Abernathy

Elevator Man: John Conwell*
*Also appeared in *Where Is Everybody?* as Air Force Colonel

Mr. Sloan: Patrick Whyte

Miss Pettigrew (listed in some sources as Miss Keevers): Nancy Rennick*
*Also appeared in *The Odyssey of Flight 33* as Paula

Crew

Producer: Buck Houghton

Director: Douglas Heyes

Director of Photography: George T. Clemens

Music: stock music used

Film Editor: Bill Mosher

Makeup: William Tuttle

Production Note

The most challenging part of this episode was getting the makeup just right.
Viewers had to perceive these actors as true mannequins to get
the full creepy effect of Marsha's true identity.

ADAPTING STORIES FROM ROD SERLING'S
THE TWILIGHT ZONE

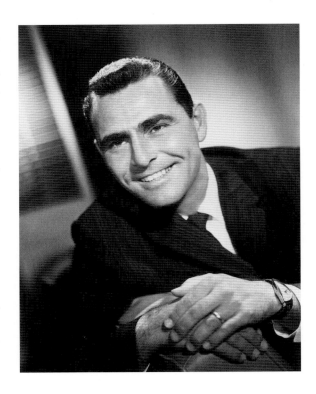

In terms of screenwriting adaptations it's trying to cut out stuff that's extraneous, without doing damage to the original piece, because you owe a debt of some respect to the original author.

—Rod Serling, 1975

At first, the idea sounded straightforward. Take an original *Twilight Zone* screenplay and adapt it into a graphic novel—break the visuals into panels, move the dialogue into balloons and captions. After all, Rod Serling himself was a fan of comics, and graphic novels are their visual and literary heirs. Serling collected Entertaining Comics titles such as *Tales from the Crypt* and *Weird Science*, the themes of which resonate in *The Twilight Zone*; even Serling's trademark narration could be considered an echo of the Crypt Keeper's introductions. Yet the more I considered the task of adapting the scripts, the more the gravity of what I was doing set in. I grew up watching *The Twilight Zone*, after all, as did so many Americans. The work required a certain reverential perspective, considering the show's iconic status, not to mention the quality of the original material.

In the 1950s the comics Serling had enjoyed were considered subversive, a threat to America's youth. Frederick Wertham published *Seduction of the Innocent* in 1954, excoriating comics in an atmosphere of public paranoia similar to a scene from *The Monsters Are Due on Maple Street*. A year later, a Senate committee was convened to investigate the pernicious influence of horror comics on America's youth, and the Comics Code Authority was established to censor comics' content. EC Comics went out of business as a direct result. In an interesting twist of fate, by the end of the decade *The Twilight Zone* was just beginning to find its television audience with stories that probably would not have made it past the comics censors. Recreating Serling's stories now, in graphic novel form, seems appropriate, emblematic of an era in which comics are finding a new readership, achieving new respect and speaking to a new audience receptive to a more sophisticated message.

Serling's stories run the gamut from serious drama, filled with fantastic and frightening dilemmas of the human condition, to wry, tongue-in-cheek humor in a sci-fi wrapper. Selecting eight as graphic novel material meant making difficult choices. Serling was a prolific writer, creating more than half of *The Twilight Zone*'s 156 scripts. It was not only a question of which of these would work best in novelized format, but which ones, as a group, would come closest to capturing the essence of *The Twilight Zone*. The stories ultimately chosen for these books possess the strongest visual possibilities and reflect an effort to achieve a cross section of Serling's dramatic range.

As I began adapting the stories for artists, I immersed myself in the screenplays and watched each episode until I felt I had internalized not just the characters, the plot, and the point, but what I imagined to be something of the author himself. In the process, I felt a growing kinship with Serling. Parts of the screenplay were often deleted from the actual show. Lines, characters, even entire scenes were struck, sometimes for budgetary reasons, sometimes because of time constraints, sometimes perhaps because Serling himself may have anticipated problems with the scenes. The show usually had only a thirty-minute time slot. The deleted scenes, however, often add richness and complexity to the story, offering a glimmer into what Serling might have done were it not for the constraints of the television medium. Restoring scenes seemed to help push the story even harder. I felt as if I were developing Serling's original design, following the telling to its logical conclusion.

With each of these stories, I have aspired to take advantage of what the graphic novel format can do. Art and text draw the reader deeply into the narrative. The reader does not just hear, but ponders, actively bridging the gaps between the panels of art with his or her own imagination. The story doesn't just happen to the reader, but, in part, *is* the reader. In other words, *The Twilight Zone* episodes had to be recreated not just to fit into a graphic novel format but to belong to it.

As much as possible, I have endeavored to keep the intentions of the original story intact—that is the "debt of respect" owed to Serling—fully functional in a new medium. From some nearby fifth dimension, I hope Serling is smiling at the prospect of these books, pleased at the thought of a new generation arriving by way of a different avenue perhaps, but entering and being welcomed into the fold of "Zonies" around the world.

—Mark Kneece
Professor of Sequential Art, Savannah College of Art and Design

Acknowledgments

Our thanks go to Carol Serling for her time and consideration while reviewing the adaptation texts and illustrated pages, and also to John Lowe, chair of the Sequential Art Department at Savannah College of Art and Design, for his assistance in pairing the right artists with the right stories.

Bloomsbury Publishing, London, Berlin and New York

First published in Great Britain in 2009 by Bloomsbury Publishing Plc
36 Soho Square, London, W1D 3QY

First published in the USA in 2008 by Walker & Company
175 Fifth Avenue, New York, NY 10010

Packaged by Design Press, a division of Savannah College of Art and Design, Inc.*
22 East Lathrop Street, Savannah, Georgia 31415, USA

Adaptation from Rod Serling's original script by Mark Kneece
Illustrated by Rebekah Isaacs
Coloring and lettering by Mia Paluzzi and Matthew Razzano
Series title treatment by Devin O'Bryan
Series copyediting by Kerri O'Hern
Series creative development by Anna Marlis Burgard and Emily Easton
Series art direction and design by Angela Rojas
Series project management by Angela Rojas and Melissa Kavonic
Creative consultant: Carol Serling

Photograph of Rod Serling © Bettmann/Corbis

A CIP catalogue record of this book is available from the British Library

ISBN 978 0 7475 8789 7

Printed in China by C & C Offset

1 3 5 7 9 10 8 6 4 2

All papers used by Bloomsbury Publishing are natural, recyclable products made from wood grown in well-managed forests. The manufacturing processes conform to the environmental regulations of the country of origin

www.bloomsbury.com/childrens
The Savannah College of Art and Design: www.scad.edu